WRITTEN BY

KATE DiCAMILLO

PICTURES BY

HARRY BLISS

JOANNA COTLER BOOKS
An Imprint of HarperCollins Publishers

To Holly McGhee
—K.D.C.

For Michelle Urry—I miss you.
—H.B.

CHAPTER ONE
Louise At Sea

LOUISE longed for adventure.
She left the henhouse and went to
sea, where the water was deep and dark.

Louise stood alone on the deck of the ship and let the wind ruffle her feathers. The sailors spoke a language she did not understand.

BLARNEY?

BLARNEY!

PIRATES!

Just as she was thinking that the sea was not quite the adventurous place she had imagined it would be, a pirate ship appeared on the horizon.

Louise watched the black-sailed ship draw near. Her heart beat fast within her feathered breast. Here, at last, was true adventure!

The pirates boarded the ship and
helped themselves to everything that
was not nailed down.

This included Louise.

"Look," shouted a one-armed pirate, "I have found a chicken!" He held Louise up high over his head.

"Fricassee the chicken, fricassee the chicken!" shouted a pirate with extremely dirty hair.

"No, no, the chicken, she must be fried," said a gold-toothed pirate.

The pirates argued heatedly about how best to consume Louise. Listening to them made Louise's heart beat alarmingly fast in her feathered breast.

"Stewed!" shouted one pirate.

"With dumplings," said another.

"Who cares how," shouted a third. "Let's just cook her!"

The pirates were still arguing when a storm began to brew.

The wind howled. Thunder boomed. Rain crashed down.
The ship was tossed about on the high seas until it cracked
in two and began to sink.

Louise saved herself by clinging to a piece of timber.

She floated past the pirate with dirty hair. He reached out for her with both hands.

"Fricasseed," he said. And then he disappeared into the mysterious ocean depths.

The wind stopped howling. The sea became calm. The sun rose.

Louise used her wings to paddle. As she worked she thought often, and quite fondly, of the warm, dry henhouse.

On her seventh day alone at sea, Louise spied land. She guided her makeshift craft to shore and hopped all the way back to the farm.

She arrived just in time for dinner.
"Where have you been, Louise?"
asked an old hen named Monique.
"Oh, here and there," said Louise.

She hopped past Monique. She went into
the henhouse and settled down in the straw.

She tucked her beak beneath her wing. She closed her
eyes; and there, safe in the warm henhouse, Louise slept
the deep and dreamless sleep of the true adventurer.

CHAPTER TWO
Louise Up High

STILL, Louise longed for adventure.
When the circus came to town,
Louise left the henhouse and followed
the bright lights and loud music.

CIRCUS

She ended up in the line for auditions.

"What is your act?"
the ringmaster asked.
Louise flapped her wings.
She clucked.
"No, no," said the ringmaster,
"what is your act?"

Louise strutted back and forth.

"Now see here," said the ringmaster. "If you want to join the circus, you must have an act."

"But, *mon cheri*," said Mitzi the aerialist, "look at her. See how she moves. She is meant, of course, to be on the high wire."

The high wire was actually quite high.

Louise walked its length carrying a pink umbrella in her beak. Far below, people clapped and cheered. Louise looked down at the world and was charmed to discover that everything had become very small.

However, too soon, walking the high wire with a pink umbrella became rather mundane, and Louise found herself longing for a little excitement.

It was then that the lion got loose.

Louise's heart beat fast within her feathered breast. Here, at last, was true adventure!

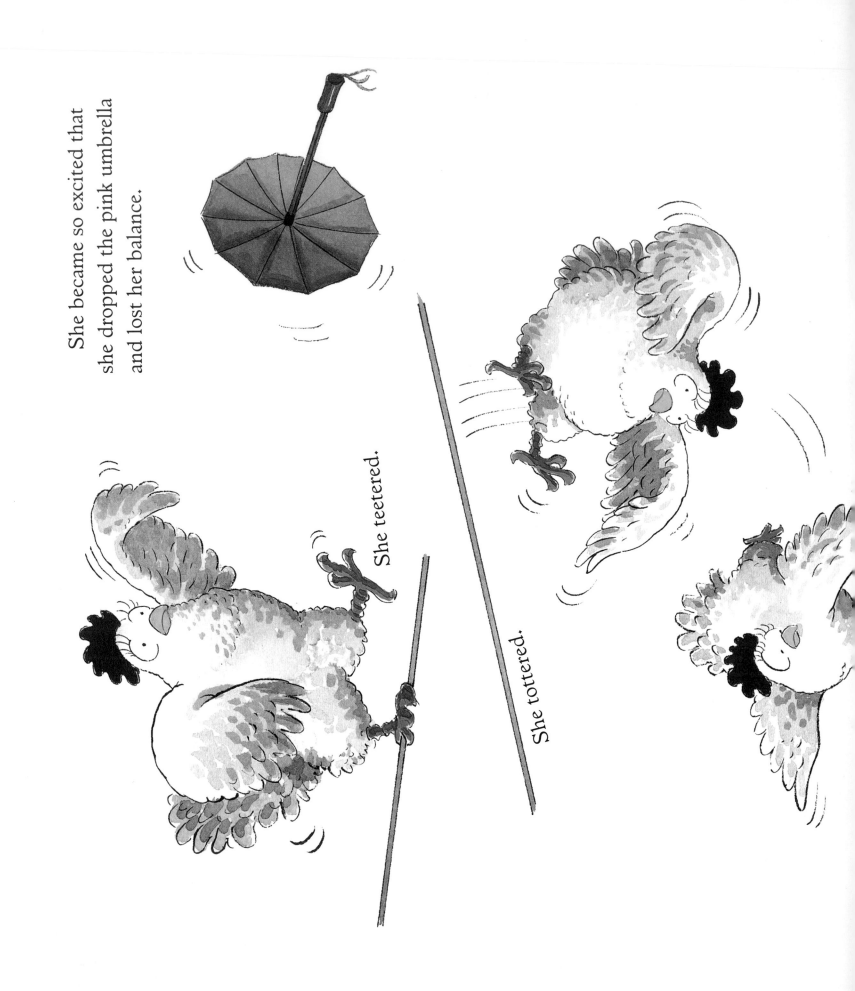

She became so excited that she dropped the pink umbrella and lost her balance.

She teetered.

She tottered.

She f e l l .

The lion positioned himself
carefully. He smacked his lips.
He opened his mouth.

Louise flapped her wings, and at the last minute, she managed to rise out of reach of the lion's jaws.

The lion roared.

The audience cheered.

Louise, her heart beating much, much too fast in her feathered breast, landed on the ground and started to run.

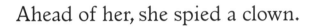

Ahead of her, she spied a clown.

She leaped atop his head. The clown put his hat on, covering Louise.

Safe in the clown's wig, hidden beneath his hat, Louise thought of the henhouse and what a quiet, spectacularly lion-free place it was.

She decided it was time to head home.

"Good-bye, my sweet *coq au vin*," called Mitzi as Louise left the circus. "Good-bye, my darling, daring chicken."

"But you can't leave," the ringmaster said. "We have just designed a most unique and death-defying act."

Louise ignored him. She hopped down the road toward home.

When she arrived back at the farm, Monique said,
"What have you been doing, Louise?"
"Oh, this and that," said Louise.

She hopped past Monique and went into the henhouse.
She settled herself comfortably in the straw. She tucked her
beak beneath her wing. She closed her eyes; and there, safe in
the warm henhouse, Louise slept the deep and peaceful sleep
of the true adventurer.

CHAPTER THREE
Louise Unbound

BUT...Louise continued to long for adventure.
She left the henhouse and journeyed to a land far away, where she discovered a fabulous bazaar.

Louise strolled the length of the market, admiring the plump tomatoes and the green asparagus, the winking jewelry and the colorful cloth. The vendors called out greetings to her, and Louise nodded politely in return.

PALM
READER

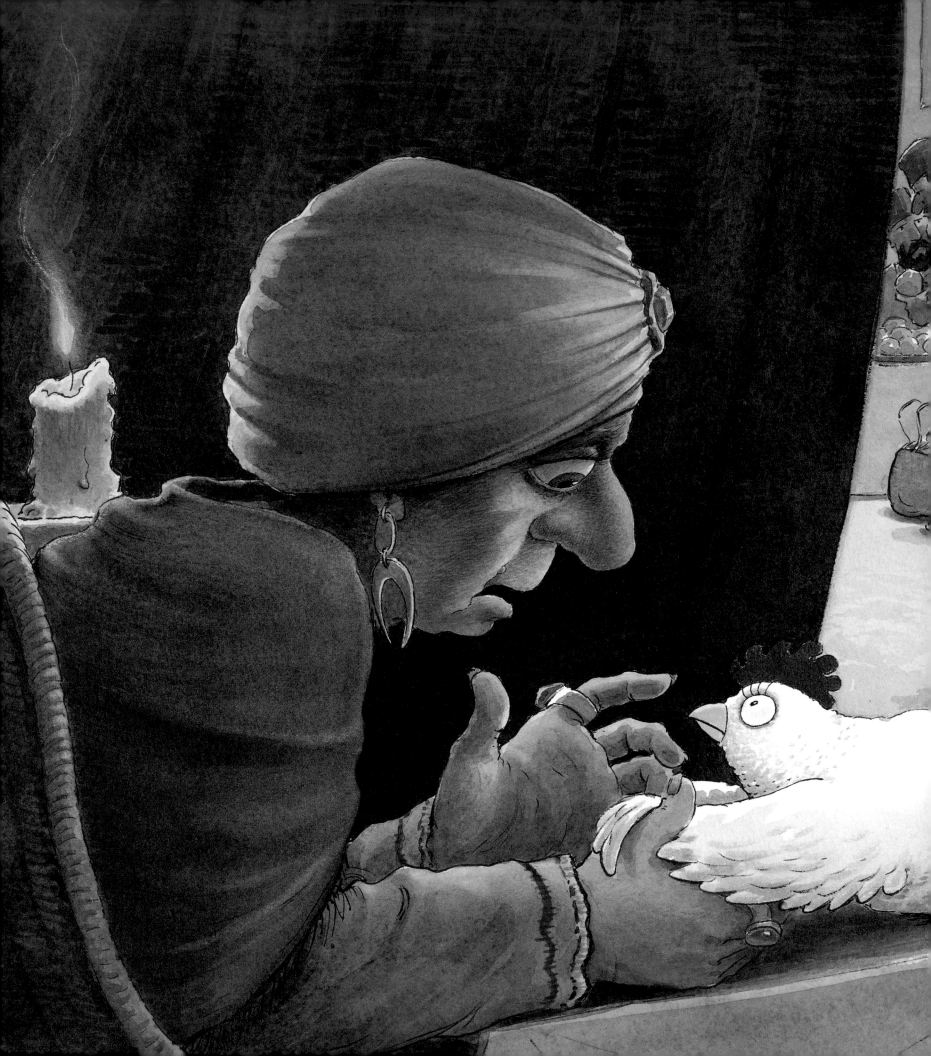

Inside a dusty purple tent, she held out her wing to a fortune-teller, who examined the feathers closely and said, in a heavily accented voice, "Hmmmm, yes. I see much adventure. I see the crossing of the seas, the walking of the wires. Also, I see the dark stranger."

PALM
READER

Louise didn't think much of this fortune, but she nodded her thanks and left the tent, where she immediately met a tall, dark stranger who swept her off her feet and shook her very hard. The man yelled at her. Louise couldn't understand what he was saying, but it was obvious that he was quite angry. Her heart began to beat fast in her feathered breast.

The man carried Louise away by her feet. Here, at last, was true adventure!

He put her in a cage that was full of
other chickens and locked the cage tight.
Louise was being held against her will!
She was a prisoner!
The other chickens did not seem to be
aware of the injustice.
Louise tried to rally them.
"Chickens do not belong in cages,"
she told them.
They looked at her.
"Chickens must roam free," she said.
The other chickens turned away from her.
Louise twisted her head out between the wires
and examined the lock. And then she set to work
picking it. Above her, the sun burned high in the sky.
As she worked, it slowly began its descent.

Finally, at dusk, Louise's
patient work paid off, and the
lock fell open with a creaky sigh.
"We are free," said Louise to the other chickens.
The news appeared to stun them.
"Free," said Louise again.
                    She hopped to the ground and
                gestured to them to follow her. One by
            one, the other chickens left the cage.

An old mud-colored hen pecked at the
hard-packed earth and gave a tentative cluck
of pleasure. Two gray hens gazed up at the
twilight sky in wonder.

Looking at them, Louise felt a wave
of longing. She missed, suddenly, her
sister hens. She missed the henhouse.
She wanted to go home.

And so she headed west, back to the farm.

At the end of her long journey, Monique was there, waiting for her. She said, "Oh, Louise, where have you been?"
And Louise looked at Monique and said, "I will tell you."

CHAPTER FOUR
And She Did

THE HENS gathered round.

They trembled as Louise told them of her adventure on the high seas. They murmured in alarm as she described the lion. They clucked in disapproval when they heard of the imprisoned chickens.

As they listened, their hearts beat fast, fast within their feathered breasts.

They said, "Oh heavens, Louise."

They said, "My goodness, Louise."

They said, "What true adventures
you have had, Louise."

"Yes," said Louise, "I have."

And when she was done with the telling,
she settled down in her nest and tucked her
beak beneath her wing. Her sister hens did the same.

Outside the henhouse it began to rain. And inside the
henhouse, safe and warm, all the chickens slept the deep
and dreamless and peaceful sleep of true adventurers.

The
End